I'm Going To **READ!**™

These levels are meant only as guides;
you and your child can best choose a book that's right.

Level 1: Kindergarten–Grade 1 . . . Ages 4–6
- word bank to highlight new words
- consistent placement of text to promote readability
- easy words and phrases
- simple sentences build to make simple stories
- art and design help new readers decode text

Level 2: Grade 1 . . . Ages 6–7
- word bank to highlight new words
- rhyming texts introduced
- more difficult words, but vocabulary is still limited
- longer sentences and longer stories
- designed for easy readability

Level 3: Grade 2 . . . Ages 7–8
- richer vocabulary of up to 200 different words
- varied sentence structure
- high-interest stories with longer plots
- designed to promote independent reading

Level 4: Grades 3 and up . . . Ages 8 and up
- richer vocabulary of more than 300 different words
- short chapters, multiple stories, or poems
- more complex plots for the newly independent reader
- emphasis on reading for meaning

LEVEL 4

Library of Congress Cataloging-in-Publication Data Available

2   4   6   8   10   9   7   5   3   1

Published by Sterling Publishing Co., Inc.
387 Park Avenue South, New York, NY 10016
Text copyright © 2005 by Harriet Ziefert Inc.
Illustrations copyright © 2005 by Barry Gott
Distributed in Canada by Sterling Publishing
c/o Canadian Manda Group, 165 Dufferin Street
Toronto, Ontario, Canada M6K 3H6
Distributed in Great Britain and Europe by Chris Lloyd at Orca Book
Services, Stanley House, Fleets Lane, Poole BH15 3AJ, England
Distributed in Australia by Capricorn Link (Australia) Pty. Ltd.
P.O. Box 704, Windsor, NSW 2756, Australia

I'm Going To Read is a trademark of Sterling Publishing Co., Inc.

Printed in China

Sterling ISBN 1-4027-2710-0

I'm Going To READ!™

Class Pets

Pictures by Barry Gott

Sterling Publishing Co., Inc.
New York

Sally

Matt

Richard

Kelly

Emily

Mr. Bunsen's Class

Mr. Bunsen

Jennifer

Jamie

Adam

Justin

Sarah

CHAPTER ONE

Surprise! Surprise!

"Good morning, class!" said Mr. Bunsen.

"Good morning, Mr. B.," said the class.

"Today is Monday," said Mr. B.

"I promised you a surprise,
 but first I have an announcement."

"Is it short?" Justin asked.

"Pretty short," Mr. Bunsen answered.

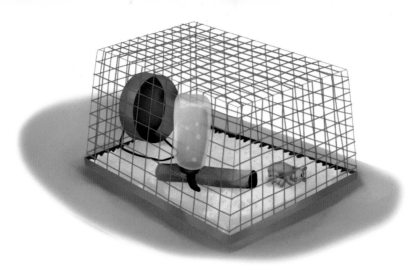

"Last night, after we left school,
one of the gerbils had babies,"
Mr. Bunsen told the class.
"Ooh! Where are they? Can I see?"
Justin asked.
"I wish they'd been born when
we were here," Kelly said.
"That would have been nice,"
said Mr. Bunsen. "But birthdays
don't always happen when you
want them to."
"That's for sure," said Kelly.
"My cousin's birthday
is on April Fool's Day."

"What do they look like?" asked Justin.

"Do they have hair?" asked Richard.

"How big are they?" asked Emily.

"Are they pink?"

"Can the babies open their eyes?"

"Can they stand?"

"Do they come from eggs?"

"Wait a minute!" said Mr. Bunsen, laughing.

"One question at a time!"

"Please, can we see the babies!"
begged Justin.

"Of course," answered Mr. Bunsen.

"But here are the rules."

Mr. Bunsen went to the blackboard.

"These rules are very important. If they
aren't followed for at least a week,
the mother gerbil might become
frightened and eat her babies."

"That's gross!" said Matt.

"I think it's sad," said Sally.

Mr. Bunsen wrote:

1. No more than two people at the cage at one time.

2. No talking or whispering near the cage.

3. HANDS OFF ALL THE GERBILS FOR 7 DAYS

"Can Emily and I have
   the first look?" asked Jamie.
"That's not fair!" said Justin.
"I asked first."
"Alphabetical order,"
   said Mr. Bunsen.
"Adam and Emily are first."

Adam and Emily went to the gerbil cage.

Mr. Bunsen kept on talking.

"We not only have four new gerbils today.

We also have five other pets."

Mr. Bunsen reached into a box on the table.

He held up a brown animal with a long tail.

"This is a kangaroo rat," he said.

From another box he pulled a lizard.

"This is a chuckwalla," he said.

"When it is scared, it puffs up with air."

Then Mr. Bunsen showed everyone
two strange-looking creatures.
He said they were desert iguanas.
He explained that *Dipsosaurus dorsalis*
is the scientific name for the desert iguana.
Matt tried saying it.
"Dip-so-saur-us dor-salis!
Sounds like a dinosaur."
"Looks like one, too," said Kelly.
"Are they related?"
"That's a good research project for you,"
said Mr. B.

Finally, Mr. Bunsen held up
a brown pocket mouse.
It was tiny, soft, and cute.
Mr. Bunsen's class was lucky.
Very lucky.
Their class was alive with animals!

"Can anyone guess what all the animals
   have in common?" asked Mr. Bunsen.
   No one guessed.
"They all live in the desert," said Mr. B.
"What are they doing here then?" Justin asked.
"We're going to build a desert," Mr. Bunsen said.
"Then we're going to put the animals
   in their new home."
"Isn't that too hard for us?" asked Adam.
"No," said Mr. B. "It's not too hard.
   I'll help you. I bought soil, sand, and plants."
"Is that all we need?" asked Matt.
"That's all," answered Mr. Bunsen.
"When do we start?" asked Sally.
"Right now!" said Mr. B.

CHAPTER TWO

Building the Desert

Mr. Bunsen brought out a special box.

It was big and deep.

Three of the sides were made of cardboard.

But the front side was clear plastic.

He put the box on a big table by the window.

Mr. B. called one group at a time
to help him build the desert.
Jennifer and Kelly were first.
They started with the dirt.
It was clean and dry.
They dumped it into the box,
one pail at a time.
It was hard work.
But it was fun.

"How much do we need?" asked Kelly.

"A lot," Mr. B. answered. "At least a foot.
  Otherwise the kangaroo rat won't burrow."

"What's burrow?" asked Jennifer.

"Burrow means he'll dig a hole
  and hide in it," said Kelly.

"Don't act so smart!" said Jennifer.

"You don't know everything!"

Richard, Matt, and Emily added the sand.
They poured it over the dirt.
"Add a little more here!" Richard yelled.
"Now put some here!" Matt shouted.
"I need some more at this end," said Emily.
Pretty soon, all of them were fighting
over who would pour where.
"Enough!" said Mr. Bunsen.
"Enough pouring. Now start mixing
the dirt and sand together."
All of them liked the feel
of the soil between their fingers.

"Do we have a foot of soil yet?"
Richard asked.

"Let's measure," said Matt.
He got a ruler.
He measured eight inches.
Not quite a foot, but almost.

"How much more soil do you
have to add?" Mr. Bunsen asked.
Matt was quick with the answer.

"Four inches!"

"That's a lot," said Emily.

"No it's not!" said Richard.

"This is fun."

"We're ready for the plants now,"
said Mr. Bunsen.
He gave Adam and Jamie work gloves.
"Planting cactus isn't easy," he said.
"They're prickly! I don't want
anyone getting stuck."
"Once I got a thorn stuck in my toe,"
said Jamie. "It hurt!"

"Watch me plant this one,"
said Mr. Bunsen. "Then you can
do the rest. Carefully."
Adam and Jamie each planted six cacti.
That made a dozen altogether.
Mr. Bunsen planted one.
Thirteen plants.
"That's called a baker's dozen,"
said Mr. Bunsen.

Sarah, Sally, and Justin had been waiting
a long time for their turn.

"I didn't mind waiting," said Sarah,
"because we have the best job.
We get to put the animals in the desert."

Mr. Bunsen showed everyone how to hold
an animal. He approached the kangaroo
rat slowly from the front, so it could see
his hand.

"This gets the animal used to your hand,"
he told the class. Then he picked up the
kangaroo rat and held it against his body.
Its feet were resting on his arm. It felt safe.

"Try not to squeeze too hard," said Mr. B.
"Even if it tries to get away.
Squeezing can make an animal afraid.
Then it might bite or run away."

"What if it wriggles a lot?" Sarah asked.

"Put your hand firmly on its back," said Mr. B.
"Firm touching calms an animal."

When Mr. B. was sure everyone understood
the difference between holding and squeezing,
he put the kangaroo rat back into the box.
Then he called Sarah, Justin, and Sally.
Sarah took the chuckwalla from its box.
She put it on her arm, just like Mr. B. had
shown them.
And do you know what?
The chuckwalla wasn't scared.
It didn't puff itself up with air!

Justin opened the box.

The first iguana was easy to catch.

"Its skin is cold," said Justin. "And scaly."

He carefully put it in the desert.

The second iguana scooted around the box.

Justin couldn't catch it.

"It's a crazy iguana!" he yelled.

"I'm scared to grab it."

"Do you want help?" Sarah asked.

"Yup," answered Justin. "I can't catch it."

The kangaroo rat was pretty big
and quite easy to hold.
Sally stroked its back.
Then she put it into the desert.
The kangaroo rat saw the iguana
and chased it around the box.
"I hope they learn to get along,"
said Sally.

Then she picked up the pocket mouse
and held it in her hand.
Its claws felt tickly.
Its fur felt silky.
Its nose wiggled when it sniffed.
The pocket mouse was so soft and cuddly.
Sally wished she could hold it
for the rest of the day.

Mr. B. attached a light to the desert wall.
"Why are you putting a light in the desert?"
asked Jennifer.
"Because our room isn't as warm
as the desert," Mr. B. explained.
"The desert gets cold at night,
so we can turn the light off
when we go home."

CHAPTER THREE

Where's the Mouse?

It was Matt's and Kelly's turn
to watch the animals in the desert.
They had pencils and paper so they could
draw pictures and make notes.
"That iguana looks comfortable," said Matt.
"He likes to be between the rock
and the heat lamp."
"The dipsosaurus dorsalis on the shady
side of the rock looks comfortable too,"
said Kelly.
"Oh, Kelly," said Matt.
"Just say IGUANA!"

Matt started to draw a picture of
the iguana warming himself near the lamp.
When the kangaroo rat came around,
the iguana jumped at him.
The rat was in the iguana's territory,
and the iguana was shooing it away.

Matt thought he would like
to hold the pocket mouse.
He looked for it all around the desert.
"Kelly," he said, "have you seen
the pocket mouse?"
"Nope," she answered.
"But I've been making notes about
the kangaroo rat.
I haven't been watching the mouse."

Matt and Kelly looked all over the desert.

Behind the rocks.

Under the cactus plants.

In the corners.

When there was nowhere else to look,

Matt yelled, "THE MOUSE IS MISSING!"

CHAPTER FOUR

Lost and Found

"What do you mean, missing?"
asked Jennifer. "It *can't* be missing!"

"But it *is*!" Matt insisted.

"You must not be looking in
the right place," said Jennifer.

"So come here and look for yourself,"
said Kelly.

Jennifer searched.

So did Emily.

Pretty soon there was a crowd at the box.

"What's going on?" asked Mr. B.

"Matt lost the pocket mouse," said Kelly.

"I did not!" said Matt.

"Okay. Okay. Calm down, Matt," said Mr. B.

"Are you sure it isn't in its burrow?"

"I didn't think of that," said Matt.
   He started to stick his finger
   down the pocket mouse's hole.
"Wait!" Mr. Bunsen stopped him.
"The mouse might bite you."
"Then how will I find him?" Matt asked.
"You'll have to think of another way,"
   said Mr. Bunsen.

Kelly had an idea.

"We could stick a piece of string
down his hole and see if he comes up."

"That might work," said Mr. Bunsen.

Matt and Kelly found a long piece
of string. They carefully put it
down the mouse's hole.

"This is like going fishing," said Kelly.

"I've never fished for
a mouse before," said Matt.

The string went down.

But the pocket mouse did not come up.

"Maybe the mouse escaped," said Adam.

"Maybe it is hiding under one of the tables
   or maybe it's under a bookcase," said Jamie.

"I hope it doesn't go outside," said Richard.

"It might freeze to death."

"I'm sure it hasn't gone that far," said Mr. B.

"Let's keep looking."

   Everyone in the class searched the room.

   Everyone but Sally.

   She stood in the corner and just watched.

Suddenly a fight broke out by the window.

Justin was pushing Matt.

"You took him!" Justin yelled.

"I DID NOT!" Matt yelled back.

"The mouse was there when it was our turn
to watch the animals," Justin shouted.

"That's enough, Justin," said Mr. Bunsen.

"I'm sure no one took the mouse.

Everyone knows the animals are for sharing."

Sally felt bad.

She didn't want Matt to get in trouble.

She wanted to talk to Mr. B. privately.

"What is it, Sally?" asked Mr. B.

"I know where the mouse is,"
  Sally whispered.

"And I'm sorry. Really sorry."

"Why are you sorry, Sally?" Mr. B. asked.

"I took the mouse," she told him.

"I put it in my backpack."

"Why did you do that?" asked Mr. B.

"It was so soft and cuddly," said Sally.

"I never had a pet of my own."

She cried so hard Mr. Bunsen gave
her two tissues for her nose.

"I'm glad you told me," he said.

"It's clear to me that you know that
what you did was wrong. Let's get
the mouse from your backpack
and take it home to the desert."

Sally wiped her eyes.

"Maybe, if your parents say yes,
you could take one of the
gerbil babies home when they're older,"
said Mr. B.

Sally smiled. "I'd like that."

She gave Mr. Bunsen the pocket mouse.

"Now remember, Sally," he told her.

"This is a pocket mouse,
not a backpack mouse!"

Sally giggled.

Mr. Bunsen knew how
to make people feel better.

"We found the pocket mouse," said Mr. B.
"Everybody back to your desks."
Mr. Bunsen put the mouse
back in the desert.
"Well, this has been quite a day,"
he said. "What did everyone learn
about pets today?"

"Be careful with pets," said Justin.

"Especially when there are babies," said Emily.

"Mice burrow," said Matt.

"Iguanas like to sun themselves," said Kelly.

"Good," said Mr. Bunsen. "Anybody else?"

"Pets are fun to share," said Sally.

"Right!" said the rest of the class.

"Well, what should we do tomorrow?"
  asked Mr. Bunsen.
"Don't YOU know?" Justin called out.
"Maybe I do, and maybe I don't,"
  Mr. Bunsen teased.

"You'll just have to wait and see.
  Class dismissed."